the MAGIC MIRROR

Big Fish, Little Fish
Text © 1989 Pippa Randolph   Illustrations © 1989 David Lewis

The Goose Girl
Text © 1989 Pete Menzies   Illustrations © 1989 Paul Demeyer

The Hobyahs
Text and illustrations © 1989 Godfrey Jones

Beauty and the Beast
Text and illustrations © 1989 Marcus Parker Rhodes

The Selkie Bride
Text and illustrations © 1989 Walter McCrorie

The Frog Prince
Text © 1989 Ragdoll Productions UK Ltd   Illustrations © 1989 Marjut Rimminen

Goldie Locks ... the Truth
Text © 1989 Jane Cottingham   Illustrations © 1989 John Cousen

The Drummer
Text © 1989 Ragdoll Productions UK Ltd
Illustrations © 1989 Valeria Petrone c/o Maggie Mundy Agency

The Story of the Devil's Bridge
Text and illustrations © 1989 Nicholas Spargo

Long, Broad and Quickeye
Text © 1989 Ragdoll Productions UK Ltd   Illustrations © 1989 Christine Roche

The Sharpest Witch
Text and illustrations © 1989 Karen Watson

Beauty Pinkerton and the Spiny Legged Wart Groveller
Text and illustrations © 1989 Tim Holmes

Jack and the Beanstalk
Text and illustrations © 1989 Alan Rogers

The 𝒦 logo is a trademark and copyright of Kellogg Company

This collection © 1989 Ragdoll Productions UK Ltd.

The illustrations and stories © remain the property of the individuals named

First published 1989 by Aurum Books for Children, 33 Museum Street, London WC1A 1LD

Printed in Great Britain by MacLehose & Partners Ltd

British Library Cataloguing in Publication Data
The magic mirror.
1. Children's stories in English
Anthologies
823'.91'0809282

ISBN 1-85406-043-0

the MAGIC MIRROR

ABC

Aurum Books for Children
London

In 1988 Ragdoll Productions organised a competition, with Kellogg as sponsor, to uncover new talent in the field of animation. Entrants were required to write and produce an animated film based on a fairy story. This book contains eleven of the winning stories in the competition in addition to two revised stories based on the originals; all are illustrated with full colour pictures, most of them from the films.

All the necessary ingredients for good fairy tales are found in this book – monsters, giants, heroes, humour, greed, mischief and magic. As well as wholly new stories such as 'The Sharpest Witch', there are traditional tales from England, Wales and Czechoslovakia, delightfully retold and sometimes placed in modern settings. A traditional 'Beauty and the Beast' sits side-by-side with a humorous version of the same story, 'Beauty Pinkerton and the Spiny-Legged Wart Groveller'; the familiar story of 'Jack and the Beanstalk' is placed in an inner city environment.

Each of these stories can, of course, be enjoyed for itself, but read in conjunction with the animated film, the full extent of the skill and creativity of the film makers becomes clear. Just as each story is unique, so is each film. The films have been made using different styles of animation, and the visual results are exciting and highly original.

Fairy tales have been entertaining people for hundreds of years, and they are enjoyed by people of all ages. This diverse collection is no exception; it will provide pleasure for everyone: children just beginning to read for themselves, parents who read aloud to young children, and adults who read for their own satisfaction.

Our film makers were:

Emma Calder and Ged Haney who chose *'The Drummer'*
John Cousen and Jane Cottingham who chose *'Goldie Locks… The Truth'*
Paul Demeyer and Pete Menzies who chose *'The Goose Girl'*
Anna Fodorova and Christine Roche who chose *'Long, Bubble and Crystal Clare'*
Tim Holmes who chose *'The Spiny Legged Wart Groveller'*
Godfrey Jones who chose *'The Hobyahs'*
Walter McCrorie who chose *'The Selkie Bride'*
Marcus Parker Rhodes who chose *'Beauty and the Beast'*
Richard Randolph and David Lewis who chose *'Big Fish, Little Fish'*
Marjut Rimminen who chose *'The Frog King'*
Alan Rogers and Peter Lang who chose *'Jack and the Beanstalk'*
Nicholas and Mary Spargo who chose *'The Story of the Devil's Bridge'*
Karen Watson who chose *'The Sharpest Witch'*

CONTENTS PAGE

Big Fish, Little Fish 6

The Goose Girl 13

The Hobyahs 23

Beauty and the Beast 29

The Selkie Bride 38

The Frog Prince 44

Goldie Locks… the Truth 51

The Drummer 61

The Story of the Devil's Bridge 72

Long, Broad and Quickeye 81

The Sharpest Witch 95

Beauty Pinkerton and the
Spiny Legged Wart Groveller 106

Jack and the Beanstalk 116

The Big Fish and the Little Fish

How the Eel came to be called Chief of all River Fish

A long, long time ago, an old blue river ran deep in the jungle of Africa. This river had once been home to hundreds of happy little fish, but now all the little fish who lived there swam in fear.

Those who swam near the great boulder at the river bend never returned, and those who swam the other way near the thick reeds saw a cruel shadow lurking.

One day the wise old fish met to talk about the great trouble that had come upon them, for they all agreed that something had to be done.

"We're trapped," said one old fish. "If we don't find a way out, we're all going to die."

The wise old fish put their heads together to ponder the

problem, but not one could come up with an answer.

"What about Little Eel," suggested one, at last. "She swims faster than any of us – in and out of everything – and she is clever even though she is small."

And so they set off to find Little Eel.

"Oh, Little Eel," said the wise old fish when they found her, "you know the trouble we are in."

"Downstream where the river bends, a giant lurks under a

slimy boulder. The other way, where the reeds are thick, is an even fiercer monster. We are trapped. What can we do?"

Little Eel listened. She knew every reed and every stone in the river, and she was clever. "There might be a way out," she told the wise old fish, "but you will need both courage and great speed."

Now, those wise old fish had never before had to be brave or quick. They put their heads together and talked before turning back to Little Eel.

"If you can save us, Little Eel," they said, "we would be honoured to make you Chief of all the River Fish."

Little Eel was pleased with this. "Now, listen to me," she said to them.

When her plan was told, Little Eel began her perilous journey towards the river bend. The water was cold and, by the time she reached the slimy boulder that was the home of the giant, there were no other fish.

"Oh great, gruesome fish!" she called out. "My master, Ruler of the River Fish, has a challenge for you!"

Silently, the mighty river bend fish slid from his home beneath the boulder. He eyed Little Eel.

"Beware!" cried Little Eel. "My master does not take kindly to having his messengers eaten by small fry like you!"

The giant's eyes opened wide in surprise. "Why ... "

"My master is tired of hearing about the bully at the river bend," Little Eel went on, bravely.

"You can tell your master," roared the giant fish, "that he'll be sorry for these insults! Tell him I am on my way!"

Little Eel had heard enough. She was off, swimming faster

than she had ever swum in her life. She passed all the other fish, who made way for her as she raced towards the narrowest part of the river where the reeds were thick and where the monster lived.

"Oh fish!" Little Eel cried. "Go quickly! Escape while you can! My master is very angry with you. He is coming to punish you!"

A monster fish, uglier than the giant fish, rose up slowly from the thick weeds. "Punish me?" he roared. "Watch your words, Little Eel!"

"My master is furious with you for eating so many of his subjects."

"His subjects! Let him come! No fish frightens me," boasted the spiny monster.

"Oh fish," pleaded Little Eel, "save yourself! Hide in the deep, thick weeds!"

"Hide?" roared the fish. "Hide!"

Little Eel saw that she had said enough. She turned tail and sped back to the other fish. "They're coming! Keep back!" she whispered. When she was sure that all the fish were hidden, she slipped into the reeds with them.

And just in time. From either side of the river came the two furious fish, teeth glinting and spines bristling.

They swam at each other and met with a blow that made the reeds bend. It was a dreadful struggle. The other fish watched as the two, locked together in their deadly battle, drifted helplessly downstream with the current.

"Little Eel, is it over?" whispered all the fish hiding amongst the reeds.

"It is over," answered Little Eel.

Then they all swam out from the reeds to celebrate their freedom.

The story of the courage and cunning of Little Eel spread all along the length of the old blue river that ran deep in the jungle of Africa.

And the wise old fish kept their word and made Little Eel Chief of all the River Fish.

The Goose Girl

Jane wanted someone to read her a story but no one was interested. The television was on, her mother was knitting, her older sister was reading a comic about her favourite rock star, Dirty Bertie, and her father was asleep on the sofa.

"Will you read me a story?" Jane asked her mother.

"Shh!" said Mum.

Jane touched her sister on the knee and her sister snapped, "No!"

Jane just looked at her father and her brother and sighed. "Okay. I'll read it myself, then." She settled down behind the sofa to read to her dog, Fudge.

"'Once upon a time there lived a Queen who had a beautiful daughter ...'

Look Fudge, the Queen looks like Mum! I'll be the beautiful Princess!

'... her daughter was engaged to a handsome Prince who lived in the Happy Land beyond the mountains ...'"

Suddenly, Jane and Fudge found themselves whisked away into a magical kingdom.

"'A handsome Prince!" cried the beautiful Princess Jane. "Whoopee!" and she disappeared, returning a moment later with suitcases bulging with clothes.

"'Bye, Mum! I'm going to marry the handsome Prince of Happy Land!"

"Wait," said the Queen. "I have a present for you."

"A present?" said Princess Jane.

"Yes! A maid and a horse."

"Hi," said the horse, who bore a strange resemblance to

her dog, Fudge.

"He talks!" cried the astonished Princess Jane.

"Of course he talks," said Falada.

"His name is Falada," said the Queen.

"Oh, thanks Mum! 'Bye!" said the Princess. She climbed on to Falada's back to begin the long journey with her maid to her bridegroom's kingdom in the Happy Land beyond the mountains.

"These cases are heavy," grumbled the maid, who bore an even stranger resemblance to Jane's older sister.

Soon they came to a beautiful oasis. "Bring me some water, please," ordered Princess Jane.

But the maid replied, "Get it yourself."

The Princess was used to her maid's bad behaviour, so she climbed from Falada's back. The water was so fresh that she threw off her clothes and leaped in. "Yippee!" she cried.

Now, while Princess Jane was swimming, the maid changed out of her own clothes into the Princess's clothes, and when Princess Jane emerged from the water, she found the maid sitting on Falada's back dressed in her clothes.

"What are you doing?" asked the Princess.

"From now on," said the maid, "I'm the Princess and you carry the cases. And if you tell a soul that I'm your maid ..."

A noisy bee flew by.

"I'll put a bee up your nose!"

Princess Jane dressed in her maid's clothes.

"Do you swear to keep silent?" demanded the maid.

"Yes," replied the Princess, sulking.

"Good. Come on – I want to meet this Prince."

"These cases are heavy," complained the Princess.

"If your mother only knew her heart would surely break in two," said Falada, shaking his head.

After many days and nights they arrived in the Happy Land. Birds were singing and the King rushed out of his palace to greet the travellers. The King bore a marked resemblance to Jane's father.

"Welcome to the Royal Palace!" said the King.

The maid jumped down from Falada and demanded, "Where's the handsome Prince?"

"Oh...er, Bertie!" called the King.

"Coming!" replied a voice.

"Listen," said Falada suddenly, "that Princess is not…"

"Er, dear King," said the maid quickly, "may I ask a favour of you?"

"Of course," replied the King.

"This horse is bewitched. Please have your men destroy him."

The handsome Prince appeared and stood beside his father.

"Rhubarb, rhubarb, rhubarb!" said Falada, rolling his eyes.

"He's got a big mouth," the Prince said.

Falada opened his mouth wide and bared his teeth.

"Falada!" said the shocked Princess Jane.

"Well, if your mother only knew it would break her heart in two," said Falada.

"What a weird horse!" said the Prince.

"Hmm," said the King. "Your wish will be granted. We will nail his head above the Palace gates."

Princess Jane and Falada looked at each other, dumbstruck.

So Falada's head was nailed above the Palace gates and Princess Jane was sent to look after the royal geese. Nobody knew her name so they called her the Goose Girl.

Each evening the Goose Girl drove the royal geese back to the Palace, and every evening she paused under Falada's head to ask, "What will become of me, Falada?"

Falada always replied, "If your mother only knew, her heart would break in two."

"Don't keep saying that!" said Princess Jane one night.

"But it's true!" said Falada.

Princess Jane began to cry.

The King appeared at the Palace gates. "What is going on? Crying is not allowed in the Happy Land. Stop it!" And then he started to cry, too. "Please stop crying!" he sobbed.

A footman approached. "Your Majesty, it's time for supper."

"Quiet everyone!" commanded the King, and the Goose Girl stopped crying at once. "It's supper time!" he announced.

Hearing this, the geese honked and ran through the Palace gates.

"Tut, tut, tears, hmmm? I want you to come with me, Goose Girl."

The King escorted the Princess to the royal apartments and, sitting on his throne, motioned for her to sit at his feet.

"Now, I want to know why you were crying. This is the Happy Land. Crying isn't allowed."

"I ... I can't tell you," said the Princess. "It's a secret."

"I see," said the King.

"I mustn't tell a soul!" said the Princess.

"Hmm," said the King. "Well then, you'd better tell the walls."

"The walls?" The Princess stopped crying.

"Oh, yes, walls have ears. A trouble shared is a trouble halved. Now, count to one hundred. I'll leave the room, and then you can tell the walls."

The Princess began to count as the King ran out the door and huffed and puffed up the stairs to the roof. He leaned

over the chimney, just in time to hear the Princess counting, "98...99...100!"

"Ready!" said the King, impatiently.

"When I left home," muttered the Princess, "to marry the handsome Prince, I was a Princess."

"Louder!" shouted the King.

She raised her voice. "Now my maid is engaged to the Prince."

"What?" roared the King, forgetting himself, and he lost his balance and fell down the chimney with a crash, landing in the fireplace covered in soot.

"Oh, er, sorry to disturb you," the King apologised. "Er, have you finished?"

The Princess giggled. "Yes."

"Good, come with me. It's supper time."

The King escorted the Princess to the royal table, where they took their places.

"Ah, there you are," said the King, seeing the handsome Prince and the maid sitting at the table.

"There's a matter I wish to discuss with the 'Princess'," said the King, turning to the maid. "I need your advice."

The maid was more interested in her food than in what the King was saying. "Hmmm?" she mumbled between mouthfuls.

"A friend of mine," said the King, "has been wronged by someone she trusted."

"Hmmm..."

"She has lost everything – her clothes, her horse, the man she loves ..."

The King continued telling the story to the maid.

"Do you want my chips?" the Princess asked the handsome Prince at the other end of the table.

"Don't you want them?" asked the Prince, surprised.

"No, I'm on a diet."

"Hey, thanks!" he said, as she scraped the potatoes on to his plate.

Meanwhile, the King was coming to the end of his story. "So," he asked the maid, "what would you do about the person who wronged my friend?"

The maid thought for a moment and said, "I'd put him in a barrel full of drawing pins and roll the barrel till he dies."

"It's not a man," said the King. "It's a maid."

At last the maid understood. She gulped.

"Yes, it's you!" roared the King. "Guard, take her away!"

The guard carried her out by the scruff of her neck, kicking and thrashing. "On second thoughts," she cried, as she was dragged away, "a barrel of drawing pins is a bit old fashioned. What about a good talking to and no sweets for a week?"

The door shut with a clang behind her.

Princess Jane and her Prince were united at last. The wedding day was arranged and all the geese were invited to join in the splendid feast.

And so they all lived happily ever after – well, nearly all ...

... the wicked maid was rolled down the hill in a barrel of drawing pins until she promised to behave.'

Jane closed the book. "That's all," she told Fudge, looking carefully at his neck. Jane popped her head up from behind the sofa. Everyone had fallen asleep in front of the television.

"Are you okay?" Jane asked her sister.

"Yes, why?" asked her sister, stretching.

"I read a story; it was really good."

"What was it about?" her sister yawned.

"A goose girl," answered Jane.

The Hobyahs

An English Folk Tale

Many years ago there was a brave black dog called Turpie. He lived with a little old man and a little old woman in a little house by the river. The little old man grew hemp to make ropes, and the little house was made of hemp. Dog Turpie looked after the little old man and the little old woman and barked loudly when anyone came near the house.

But deep in the woods lived the Hobyahs. They had long fingers and long noses and ran on the ends of their long pointed toes. The Hobyahs slept all day, but when it was dark they came running, creeping through the long grass and skipping along on the ends of their long pointed toes.

One night when the little old man and the little old woman were fast asleep, out from the deep woods, run, run, running came the Hobyahs. Through the long grass, creep, creep, creeping came the Hobyahs. Skip, skip, skipping on the ends of their long pointed toes came the Hobyahs.

They cried, "Pull down the hemp stalks! Eat up the little old man. Carry off the little old woman!"

But brave Dog Turpie jumped up and down, barking loudly.

The Hobyahs were afraid. They ran home again as fast as they could go.

But the little old man woke up and said, "Dog Turpie jumps up and down and barks so loudly that I cannot sleep. Tomorrow night I will tie up his legs."

So the next night when it was bedtime, the little old man tied up Dog Turpie's legs. Then he went to bed.

Out from the deep woods, run, run, running came the

Hobyahs. Through the long grass, creep, creep, creeping came the Hobyahs. Skip, skip, skipping on the ends of their long pointed toes came the Hobyahs.

They cried, "Pull down the hemp stalks! Eat up the little old man! Carry off the little old woman!"

Brave Dog Turpie barked loudly.

The Hobyahs were afraid. They ran home again as fast as they could go.

But the little old man woke up and said, "Dog Turpie barks so loudly that I cannot sleep. Tomorrow night I will tie up his mouth."

So the next night when it was bedtime, the little old man tied up Dog Turpie's mouth. Then he went to bed.

Now poor Dog Turpie could not jump or bark. There was no one to frighten the Hobyahs.

That night when the little old man and the little old woman were fast asleep, out from the deep woods run, run, running came the Hobyahs. Through the long grass, creep, creep, creeping came the Hobyahs. Skip, skip, skipping on the ends of their long pointed toes came the Hobyahs.

They pulled down the hemp stalks.

They ran past brave Dog Turpie and into the house. The little old man hid under the bed but the Hobyahs seized the little old woman, put her in a bag, tied the top and dragged her all the way home.

The Hobyahs hung the bag on a big hook. Then they poked it with their long fingers and cried, "Look you, look you!"

And when the sun came up, they went to sleep.

When the little old man found the little old woman was gone, he was very sorry. He realised how good and brave Dog Turpie had been. So he untied Turpie's legs and mouth and set him free.

Then Turpie went sniffing and snuffing along to find the little old woman. He sniffed along the fields and through the long grass, and snuffed along the hedges, until he came to the deep woods.

Soon he came to the Hobyahs' house.

He heard the little old woman crying in the bag. He saw that the Hobyahs were all fast asleep. Then Dog Turpie cut open the bag with his sharp teeth.

Out jumped the little old woman. She ran home as fast as she could.

But brave Dog Turpie did not run away. He crept inside the bag to hide.

When night came, the Hobyahs woke up. They went to the big bag and poked it with long fingers. They cried, "Look you, look you!"

Out of the bag jumped brave Dog Turpie. He ate up every one of the Hobyahs.

And that is why the little old man and the little old woman and Dog Turpie were never troubled again, and why there are no Hobyahs alive today.

Beauty and the Beast

A fat and prosperous merchant stood by his horse, surrounded by his three daughters. "I'm sorry to have to leave you for so long," he said, "but if there is anything you want, I will bring it home with me."

"Anything at all?" asked the first daughter excitedly. "Promise?"

"Anything you want, I promise," said the merchant.

"Then bring me pearls!" cried the first daughter.

"Pearls?" gasped the merchant. "Look, I didn't mean ..."

"You promised!" said the second daughter. "You did! And I want a silk dress."

"Oh bother," said the merchant. "All right then." He looked at his youngest daughter and said crossly, "Well, Beauty, what about you?"

"Just bring me a rose, Daddy," said the lovely girl. "That's all I want."

The merchant gave her a kiss and then, saying farewell, he mounted his horse and set off on his journey.

It was a cold winter's day and the countryside looked bleak. As the merchant passed by a high wall he suddenly saw red roses hanging over. He stopped and found that by standing on his horse, he could just scramble to the top of the wall. Unsteadily, he leaned over and plucked a rose but, in doing so, he lost his balance and fell over the wall on to the other side.

The merchant sat up and found himself in a fabulous garden. Despite the bleak winter's day, it seemed to be spring. The merchant checked his plucked rose for damage, and then gazed up at the wall in despair. It was far too high to climb.

Suddenly, a huge, hairy hand fell on his shoulder and a voice called, "Thief!"

"Help!" cried the merchant as he turned. "Oh! What horrible thing are you?"

"I'm just a wizard," said the Beast. "A rival has turned me into the Beast you see before you. We had an argument."

The Beast pulled the merchant to his feet and began marching him through the garden. "Now, off to prison with you, thief!"

"Wait!" cried the merchant. "It was only a rose, your honour."

"Of course," said the Beast, slowing down, "there is something you can give me in return."

"There is?" said the merchant. "It's yours! Um, what, exactly?"

"I want the first thing of yours that you see upon your return home."

"The first thing of mine ..."

"... that you see upon your return home."

The merchant thought hard. "All right!" he said finally. "Fine! It's yours! Whatever it is ... but please, let me go."

The Beast let go of him. "Take your rose and go!" he

commanded. "But no tricks, now. I shall be watching you!"

The beast led him to the main gate and the merchant hurried back to his horse, looking nervously behind him.

It was a far harder promise to keep than the merchant had realised. The first thing that he saw as he approached home was his third daughter, Beauty, who had walked out to meet him.

"But why me, Daddy?" she asked when he had explained his promise to her. "It's ridiculous!"

"He planned it that way. I'm sure of it!" said the merchant angrily, stroking his chin.

"But I'm your daughter!" wailed Beauty.

The merchant tried to explain to her. "He's a sorcerer, my dear, a wizard! You don't fool around with people like that."

"Is he very ugly?"

"But very rich, dear," the merchant assured her.

So the merchant took his youngest daughter to the Beast's palace to fulfill his promise. As they approached, the great iron gates swung open and, leaving winter behind, they rode through the fabulous gardens towards a fairy-tale palace. The Beast was waiting for them at the top of the staircase.

"So you have kept your word, Sir," he said to the merchant.

Beauty took one look at the Beast and hid her face. "Oh Daddy, how could you?" she sobbed. "It's a hideous Beast!"

"Don't worry, Sir," said the Beast. "I'll take the best care of her. Come, my dear, I shall show you to your room. Farewell, Sir!"

And he led Beauty to the top of the stairs and through the

palace door. "Daddy!" cried Beauty, but the door had closed behind them.

"Goodbye!" called the merchant. "Don't forget to write!" He stood for a moment, and then rode sadly home.

Inside the palace, the Beast opened Beauty's bedroom door and showed her in. "Oooh!" said Beauty, forgetting her unhappiness for a moment as she looked at the wonderful room with the four-poster bed that was to be hers.

"I hope you'll find it comfortable," began the Beast, but Beauty began to cry again. "Beast! Monster!"

The Beast opened a wardrobe which was full of beautiful dresses. "These are for you," he said kindly. "Our dinner is waiting downstairs. Come down when you are ready," and he left Beauty alone.

"Oh, Daddy, how could you?" she whispered. And she turned to the wardrobe and looked through the dresses.

Even though the dining room was magnificently appointed, and the table was spread with a banquet and lit by candles, the sight and noise of the Beast's dreadful table manners upset Beauty.

"You're not eating, my dear," said the Beast. "Aren't you at all hungry?"

Beauty put her hands over her ears and ran from the room.

The next morning, she was awoken by a knock at the door. "Good morning!" called the Beast outside the door. "I hope you slept well?"

"Go away!" cried Beauty. She looked around the room for a place to hide and, seeing another door, ran through it.

She continued running down an oak-panelled hall and into a library filled with great leather-bound books. Beauty stopped in wonder and began to look along the shelves. She took down a small book called 'Magic for Beginners' and sat down to read it. She was so busy reading that she did not notice the Beast enter the library and stand behind her chair, watching her. She went on practising gestures from the book.

"Not like that, like this!" said the Beast at last and, flinging out a hand, there was a cloud of gold dust and a flock of butterflies fluttered from his palm. Beauty laughed and tried again and this time she, too, made magic butterflies.

"I did it! It works!" she cried. Then he showed her another magic trick, and another, and together they went through the book and practised all the spells.

That evening, as they sat at the dinner table, Beauty sat picking at her food and listening to the awful noise from the Beast as he ate. Finally she threw down her fork and glared at him. "You have the beastliest table manners imaginable!" she cried. "I can't bear it."

"I do apologise, my dear," said the Beast looking embarrassed. "I find eating a bit difficult with all these teeth."

Beauty got up and walked around the table. She sat down next to the Beast, took up his fork and commanded him to open his mouth. Then she spoon-fed him the rest of his dinner.

Several weeks passed, with Beauty learning magic spells during the day and feeding the Beast his dinner every evening. One day, Beauty and the Beast were walking together in the garden when Beauty sighed.

"Aren't you happy, dear?" asked the Beast kindly.

"Beast! Kidnapper!" cried Beauty. "I want to go home."

"But I'm under this curse," explained the Beast patiently. "Without you I should weaken and decline. I need you here."

"Couldn't I go on just a little visit? Just for a few days?" she begged.

The Beast thought for a while. "Seven days without you and I shall be dead."

"I shall be back in seven days, I promise! It would make me so happy. Sir? Please?"

The Beast could not refuse. He stood at the palace door and watched her leave. "Remember!" he said. "For seven days only! You must be back here on the seventh day, or I will die."

"Of course I will," she promised, "Don't worry. I'll be back in time," and she set off through the gates, waving.

The Beast went back into the palace and waited. Six days came and went and Beauty did not return. The palace looked very different now. It lay in ruins with dust and cobwebs in every room. On the seventh day the Beast, dressed only in rags, sat gazing into his crystal ball. "Where are you, Beauty?" he whispered. "Your time is up!" In the ball he could see Beauty sitting around a piano at home with her sisters. "She promised me ..!"

At last Beauty's carriage drew up outside the iron gates. She ran up the steps into the ruined palace, unable to believe what she saw. "Where are you?" she cried frantically, searching for the Beast in every room. At last Beauty found the Beast in the library, lying on the ground as if he were dead. Kneeling beside him, she lifted his head into her lap.

"Oh you poor thing!" she cried. "Don't die! I'm sorry I'm late. I didn't mean it. It's all my fault. Wake up, my love!"

Beauty kissed his hairy face — and suddenly the Beast was transformed into a young magician!

"You came back," he said, opening his eyes. "I really thought you weren't coming."

"You faker!" said Beauty. "Why didn't you do that before?"

The young magician glanced around the room and, with a magical gesture, transformed the room to its former glory.

"I was cursed, remember?" he explained. "I couldn't break the spell that made me into a Beast. Only a kiss from a true love could do that."

"True love," said Beauty, blushing. "Do you mean me?"

"You! Who else, my love?" smiled the magician.

Beauty looked at him. "You were a splendid Beast," she laughed. "Can you change back sometimes?"

And she took his hand.

The Selkie Bride

On cold, dark nights, villagers from the crofts around the coasts of Scotland gather round their firesides and tell each other tales of long ago – tales of strange creatures, who lived in the waters of the sea. Sometimes, it seems to the storytellers that they can see the strange forms, swimming in the flickering flames of the fire.

One tale tells of three brothers. One night, when the sea was calm, they went fishing together. It was a warm, moonlit night and their oars slid quietly through the dark, brooding water. As they came around an outcrop of land, they saw some figures on the beach before them. It was a group of girls, laughing and dancing in the moonlight.

The brothers pulled their boat quietly on to the shore and crept behind some rocks to watch. The youngest brother, Codrum, noticed one girl unlike any he had ever seen before. He could not take his eyes from her. She danced lightly on her toes and her black hair gleamed in the moonlight. She had smooth, olive skin and her dark, shining eyes were as mysterious and beautiful as the moon on the dark waters of the sea.

"Come, follow me," his eldest brother whispered, and they crept towards a pile of sealskin caps lying on the sand.

"Take one," he said, "and tonight you shall have a bride." Codrum did not understand but, as his brothers each picked up a cap, so did he. Then they all crept back behind the rocks to watch.

When the sun began to rise, the girls collected their caps and ran to the sea, pulling their caps on their heads as they dived into the water. As they disappeared from sight, they

seemed to Codrum to look more like fish or seals than girls.

Soon only three remained, searching frantically for their caps on the beach.

"Where are they?" cried one. "Where can they be?"

"Here!" Codrum turned to see his eldest brother standing with one of the caps in his hand. "I have your cap and I claim you as my bride. For I know that you are Selkies, seals in human form, and I know that you cannot return to the sea as long as I have your seal cap."

One Selkie came meekly towards him and knelt at his feet. "You are right," she said. "You have my cap and I will be your bride, as I must."

The second brother stepped forward and he, too, claimed his bride.

Codrum motioned to the girl he had been watching all night. "Is this yours?" he asked, holding out a cap. She nodded.

"Then you will be my bride and my love will be greater than all the oceans of the world." And he took her hand and kissed her, and led her away from the sea.

Later that day the brothers, who were worried that their brides might find their caps and return to the sea, hid the seal caps from the girls.

Codrum was hiding his in a cliff overlooking the shore, when he noticed his bride sitting alone on the rocks below, gazing at the water. He stopped and smiled, for he loved her dearly, and began to climb quietly down the rocks to surprise her. But, as he got closer, he heard her softly singing.

"What is that song?" he asked. "And why is it so sad?"

"I am singing to the sea," she replied. "I know that you love me, and would do nothing to hurt me, but the sea is my home and my heart can never leave it."

And she told him about her life in the sea; about the great blue whales that move through the oceans like mountains, and how they leap into the air and land with a great crash, sending foam and spray high into the sky. And about the beautiful ice cathedrals of the North, where the Selkies play, darting through the great tunnels and columns of moulded ice. And of swimming through great coloured shoals of fish, like flying through the heart of a rainbow.

As she spoke, Codrum could imagine her there, swimming free. And in his heart he felt her joy and wonder at being part of the sea.

Codrum felt a drop of water on his hand and, looking up, saw that his bride was crying. He held her in his arms and in her sobs he heard all the sorrows of the world, and he felt as if his heart were breaking, for he knew that she would never be his; she would always belong with the sea.

Codrum's heart was heavy as he returned the cap to his bride and watched her walk slowly down to the shore, diving without a ripple into the ocean.

Night after night Codrum sat alone by the sea. He almost wished he and his brothers had never seen the Selkies, for they had lost their brides and it had brought them only sorrow.

One Selkie had found her cap as her husband lay sleeping, and in the morning she was gone.

When the other brother heard this he grew afraid, for he loved his bride. While she was in the house he tried to burn

the seal cap, but she saw him and came running out to save it. She threw herself into the flames and was lost.

So it was that Codrum sat alone, staring into the sea, thinking of his bride. He missed her sad, dark eyes and her strange, soft song. It seemed as though he could hear her song again in the sounds of the wind, as sad and lonely as his heart.

He was so lost in his thoughts that he didn't see the ripples of the water or hear the footsteps moving gently up the shingle towards him.

"Codrum."

He looked up, startled, and there before him was his bride, dark and lovely in the moonlight.

"Codrum," she said, "I have been watching you from the

sea, and I have missed you. Although I must return to the sea, I will join you here by the rocks every ninth night as your bride. And our love will be greater than all the oceans."

And she took him gently by the hand and together they slipped quietly into the dark waters of the night.

For years people talked of seeing a couple walking together in the moonlight; until there came a day when they were seen no more. Some said the man had become a Selkie, too, and joined his bride in the sea. Some said that she had joined him on the land as his wife. And others spoke of seeing strange, dark children with smooth, olive skin and sleek, black hair, and soft, dark eyes that seemed to hold all the magic and mystery of the oceans.

The Frog Prince

A princess walked one evening in a wood. She sat down by a cool spring of water and amused herself by tossing a ball in the air and catching it as it fell. It was a golden ball, her favourite plaything, and she preferred it above all her other possessions.

After a while, she threw it so high that, when she stretched out her hand to catch it, the ball bounced away and fell into the spring. The princess looked down into the water but it was very deep – so deep that she could not see the bottom.

She began to cry and said, "Alas! If I could only have my ball again, I would give in return all my fine jewels and everything I have in the world!"

As she spoke, a frog put its head out of the water and said, "Princess, why do you weep so bitterly?"

"You cannot help me, you nasty frog," said the princess. "My golden ball has fallen into the spring."

The frog replied, "I heard you promise jewels. I do not want them, but if you will love me and let me live with you, if you will allow me to eat from your little golden plate and sleep upon your little bed, I will bring you your ball again."

"What nonsense this frog talks!" thought the princess. "He cannot get out of the spring. However, he may be able to get my ball for me, so I will promise him what he asks." So she said to the frog, "Very well, then. If you will bring me my ball, I promise to do all you require."

Then the frog put his head down, and dived deep under the water. After a little while, he came up with the ball in his mouth, and threw it on the ground. As soon as the young princess saw her ball, she ran to pick it up. She was so overjoyed to have it again that she never thought of the frog, but ran home with it as fast as she could. The frog called after her, "Stay, princess, and take me with you as you promised!" But she would not stop to listen.

The next day, just as the princess sat down to dinner, she heard a strange noise, flip-flap, as if something were coming up the marble staircase, and soon afterwards something knocked gently at the door, and said,

"Open the door, my princess dear,
Open the door, thy true love is here!
Remember the promises that were made
By the fountain cool in the greenwood shade."

Then the princess ran to the door and opened it, and there she saw the frog whom she had quite forgotten. She was frightened and, shutting the door as fast as she could, came back to her seat. The king, her father, asked her what had frightened her. "There is a nasty frog at the door," she said. "He brought me my ball when it fell into the spring yesterday. I promised him, as a reward, that he should live with me here, thinking that he could never get out of the spring — but there he is at the door and he wants to come in!"

While she was speaking the frog knocked again at the door and said,

"Open the door, my princess dear,
Open the door, thy true love is here!
Remember the promises that were made
By the fountain cool in the greenwood shade."

The king said to the young princess, "As you have made a promise, you must keep it. Go and let him in." She did so, and the frog hopped into the room and came up close to the table.

"Pray lift me up. Put me on a chair," said he to the princess, "and let me sit next to you."

As soon as she had done this, the frog said, "Put your plate closer to me that I may eat out of it."

This she did, and when he had eaten as much as he could, he said, "Now I am tired; carry me upstairs and put me into your little bed."

The princess took him in her hand and put him upon the pillow of her own little bed, where he slept all night long. As soon as it was light, he jumped up, hopped downstairs, and went out of the palace. "Now," thought the princess, "he is gone, and I shall be troubled by him no more."

But she was mistaken; for when night came again, she heard the same tapping at the door and, when she opened it, the frog was there once again. "I gave my promise," sighed the princess and allowed the frog to come in and sleep upon her pillow as before, until the morning came.

The third night he did the same, but when the princess awoke the next morning, the frog was no longer there. Instead, she was astonished to see a handsome prince standing at the head of her bed, gazing at her with the most beautiful eyes she had ever seen.

He told her that he had been put under an enchantment by a malicious fairy who had changed him into a frog. It had been his fate to remain in that form until a princess let him sleep upon her bed for three nights. "You," said the prince,

"kept your promise and broke this cruel spell, and now I have nothing to wish for but that you should go with me into my father's kingdom, where I will marry you, and love you as long as you live."

The young princess was not long in giving her consent and, as they spoke, a splendid carriage drove up with eight beautiful horses in golden harnesses, decked with plumes of feathers. Behind rode the prince's servant who had bewailed the misfortune of his dear master so long and bitterly that his heart had almost burst.

Then they all set out, full of joy, for the prince's kingdom, where they arrived safely, and lived happily ever after.

Goldie Locks ... the Truth

Goldie sat with her feet on the desk of her office tossing sweets into the air and catching them in her mouth. On the glass door of the office were the words 'Goldie Locks Toy Detective Agency'. It had been a long morning and so far there were no cases. Suddenly, the telephone rang; Goldie answered.

"Hi!" she said. "Goldie Locks Toy Detective Agency! You have a problem, I can solve it. You have a mystery, I can solve it. What have you got?"

Goldie waited for the answer.

"Your house is in a mess? You don't need a detective agency, Duckie; you need a cleaning agency."

Again Goldie paused to hear the voice at the other end.

"You don't know who did it? Okay, I'm coming over. The three bears' house?"

"I'll bear that in mind."

In no time Goldie was out the door and winding up her toy plane that she used to get around.

Soon she was walking towards the three bears' house, case in hand. What Goldie did not realise, as she tossed another sweet into her mouth, was that a dark, mysterious figure was watching her from behind a tree. It was Miss Bunyon, and she was holding a bag of shoes. "Ha! Goldie Locks the toy detective! She's the last person on earth I'd choose for a case!" and she cackled as she scurried away.

Meanwhile, Goldie had reached the bears' front door. Only Baby Bear's toy duck was at home.

"What's up, Duck?" asked Goldie.

"Thanks for coming, Goldie Locks," said Duck. "I'm

relying on you to quack the case. The three bears went out to get some honey and a mysterious, dark stranger came in and look what happened!"

At that moment, Miss Bunyon crashed through the front door. She stepped right on Duck, who quacked loudly, and then she tore through the house, wildly throwing everything in sight into the air. Then she was gone as fast as she had come, once more stepping on Duck, who quacked loudly, in her rush to get out the door.

"Looks like foul play," Goldie said to Duck, not noticing the interruption.

"I guess that makes me a prime suspect," said Duck nervously.

"So, someone breaks in and roughs up the house," said Goldie. "Someone who's about as smooth as a square mile of sandpaper. Whoever did this must have left some clues."

Goldie pulled a magnifying glass out of her toy briefcase and peered through it into the porridge bowl.

"They even ate Baby Bear's porridge!" squawked Duck.

"So ... we're looking for someone with no style — and even less taste," stated Goldie flatly. "I'll make Baby Bear some more porridge when he comes home."

Goldie prowled around the kitchen with her magnifying glass until she came to a suitcase. She opened it. Inside was a joint of beef.

"I see someone's already cased the joint!" she told Duck.

"And look at Baby Bear's little chair!" added Duck, pointing to what had once been a chair, blowing in the breeze.

"That's some rocking chair," responded Goldie. "I'd

better look upstairs for clues."

"But mind how you go!" warned Duck. "The doors are quite low. Don't forget to duck!"

Goldie carefully climbed the stairs. But she tripped over a little red shoe, banged her head on the bed post and landed, unconscious, on Baby Bear's bed.

At that moment the front door flew open. The three bears were home.

Daddy Bear came in first and stepped on Duck, who quacked loudly. He was followed by Mummy Bear. She stepped on Duck, who quacked loudly. Baby Bear came last; he stepped on Duck, who quacked loudly.

The bears walked round their chairs.

"Whooo's been sitting in my chair?" asked Daddy Bear.

"Whoo's been sitting in my chair?" asked Mummy Bear.

"And who's been sitting in my chair – and broken it all into pieces!" cried Baby Bear.

The three bears walked round the table.

"Whooo's been eating my porridge?" asked Daddy Bear.

"Whoo's been eating my porridge?" asked Mummy Bear.

"And who's been eating my porridge – and eaten it all up!" cried Baby Bear.

The three bears ran up the stairs into the bedroom, where Goldie Locks lay on the bed.

"Oooooh!" they all growled angrily.

"Now I know who sat on my chair!" said Daddy Bear.

"Now I know who tried my porridge!" said Mummy Bear.

"Now I know who ate all my porridge and broke my chair

and now ... she's sleeping in my bed!" said Baby Bear.

Goldie woke up to find three angry faces staring down at her.

"Grr!" went Daddy Bear.

"Grr!" went Mummy Bear.

"Grr!" went Baby Bear.

Goldie jumped up and ran to the door but, once again, she tripped over the little red shoe.

"Aha!" she cried. "A clue, and it's been there all the time,

staring me in the toe-caps!"

She picked up the shoe and threw it in her case as she ran downstairs and out of the house, chased by three angry bears.

Duck stepped out of Goldie's way, swerved neatly out of Daddy Bear's way and side-stepped out of Mummy Bear's way. He turned to watch them and Baby Bear stepped on him. Duck quacked loudly.

Goldie wound up her toy plane and took off, her briefcase jumping about beside her.

Back in her office, Goldie sat with the briefcase in front of her. "I can see this isn't going to be an open and shut case," she said thoughtfully, tossing a sweet in the air and catching it in her mouth. "There must be a catch somewhere."

She opened the case and the red shoe jumped out and

kicked her in the shin.

"Ow!" she yelled, and began chasing it around the office. Finally she stamped on it and picked it up.

"I have a hunch this is all tied up somehow," she said, examining the laces closely. "Maybe it is and maybe it's 'knot'. If I hold on to this shoe, it could give me a lead."

Again the shoe leaped from her hand, but this time she held on to the laces and, as if it were a dog on a lead, the shoe darted off, dragging Goldie with it. It darted out of the office, down the road, across the lake, over a cliff and down a mountain, but Goldie did not let go of the lead. "I'm beginning to think we're getting somewhere!" cried the brave toy detective.

At last the shoe came to a halt outside Miss Bunyon's Academy of Nasty Dancing.

"Of course!" cried Goldie. "I should have guessed." She peered in the window. Miss Bunyon was performing a particularly nasty dance in the middle of the room, but what really drew Goldie's attention was an enormous pile of shoes at one end of the room. There, at the bottom of the pile, was the partner to the little red shoe she was holding in her hand.

Miss Bunyon stopped dancing and began talking to her own reflection in the practice mirror. "Hah hah! My plan can't fail! I have stolen shoes from nearly everyone in the world. Soon everybody will have sore feet from walking without shoes. Nobody will be able to dance anymore. Except for me! Hah hah! I will be the best dancer in the world – I will be the only dancer in the world! And I'll be rich! And famous! Then they'll all love me!"

"So that's your plan!" Goldie's reflection appeared in the mirror behind Miss Bunyon.

"Goldie!" Miss Bunyon spun around. "What are you doing here? How did you find me?"

Goldie Locks pointed to the two red shoes, reunited and jumping up and down with delight.

"That shoe was the clue that led me to you," she said.

"I left a clue?" whispered Miss Bunyon.

"You left a left shoe!" said Goldie triumphantly.

"We've got a right one here," said Miss Bunyon to herself. Goldie picked up a ballet pump.

"So! You're going to pump me for information?" asked Miss Bunyon.

"I don't have to, Miss Bunyon," answered Goldie complacently. "I know everything. But the three bears still think it was me that wrecked their house. They don't know it was you who took their place apart, looking for shoes. It's time you learned to toe the line. Come on. You've got a lot of explaining to do."

"I know this is going to sound corny," Miss Bunyon began, but Goldie grabbed her and stuffed her into her case. Then she headed back to her office and the aeroplane and they flew to the three bears' house. Without knocking, Goldie Locks flung open the door.

"I'll open the case and show you exhibit number one!" cried Goldie, doing so with a flourish. Miss Bunyon crawled out of the case.

"Miss Bunyon! So it was you!" cried Mummy Bear.

"Curses!" yelled Miss Bunyon. "I thought I turned this

place inside out!"

"Yes, but it was a mistake to come to this house," said Goldie Locks.

"I know that now," moaned Miss Bunyon. "I couldn't find a shoe anywhere."

"Of course not!"

"But why? Why?"

"'Paws' a moment, and think ..." urged Goldie.

The three bears held up their feet as the toy detective explained, "Because in this house they're always bear-footed!"

Miss Bunyon began to tear out her hair and jump up and down until, at last, she disappeared in a puff of smoke.

Just then the door that Goldie had flung open in her haste to get in, swung shut. A flattened Duck fell over. Goldie looked at the three bears, and they all laughed as Duck quacked loudly.

The Drummer

Once, a long time ago, there was a Drummer in the Queen's army who was on his way back to join his regiment. One evening he stopped to rest by the seashore before continuing his journey the next day. As he strolled by the sea, there on the sand he saw a dress of the finest linen. "There is no one to be seen," he thought. "Maybe it's been washed ashore." So he picked up the dress and put it in his pack.

That night, just as the Drummer was falling asleep, he felt as though something were flitting above his head and criss-crossing over his bed. Now, the Drummer was not easily frightened, so he called out in the dark, "Who are you? What do you want?"

"Give me back my dress!" replied a voice. "The one you found on the seashore."

"Only if you tell me who you are."

"Alas, I am the daughter of a mighty king, fallen into the hands of a witch. She has imprisoned me here in her evil kingdom. Please give me back the dress. Now the witch is drawing me back to the Glass Mountain. Her spells are strong; please give me the dress!"

The Drummer readily gave back the dress but, as the Princess snatched it and would have hurried away, he stopped her. "Wait! I will help you, I promise. Where is this Glass Mountain?"

"I dare not tell you more except that the way is long and dangerous and lies through the large forest where the Giants are," said the Princess and, in a moment, she was gone from his sight.

Next day the Drummer awoke with the sun and determined to discover whether there were, indeed, Giants or a Glass Mountain. His memory of the Princess was so clear, he could not believe it was only a dream. So he put on his drum and his pack and set off fearlessly through the forest.

He walked and he walked but saw nothing unusual. "Aha," he thought. "If there are any Giants, they are sleeping." So he took out his drumsticks and began to drum. Loudly he drummed and louder, until the whole forest echoed and at last a Giant awoke.

"How!" roared the Giant. "You wretched ant — what are you drumming here for, waking me from my sleep!"

"I am drumming," said the Drummer, "to show the way for the peasants who are following after me. My drum is the signal. They are coming with scythes and steel hammers to cut a path through this forest and they will beat out the brains of any who try to stop them."

The Giant was terribly frightened to hear all this. Wolves and bears he could deal with, but thousands of these tiny ant-like men would swarm all over him and give him no peace. He decided to make a treaty with the Drummer.

"Here, Drummer," he called. "What can I do to get you and your men to leave me in peace?"

"Show me the way to the Glass Mountain," said the Drummer, "and I will beat a retreat so our army will turn and follow another path."

"Come on then," said the Giant, "and I will carry you on my shoulder."

And so they set off with the Drummer sitting on the Giant's shoulder beating his drum with might and main and the Giant thinking all the time that the Drummer was beating a retreat.

After a while, the first Giant came to the end of his territory and handed the Drummer to a second Giant, for the Glass Mountain was still far distant.

The second Giant put the Drummer in his button-hole and there the Drummer hung on to the Giant's button, which was as big as a dinner plate. He looked around him in high spirits, for it seemed to him the Giant's strides were covering the ground at a marvellous pace.

Very soon they came to the end of that Giant's ground and the Drummer was passed to a third Giant who placed him in his hat. This was the best of all, for the Drummer could walk all around the brim and view the countryside from every angle. From there he could see, on the horizon, the shining peak of the Glass Mountain. Three more giant strides and they arrived at its foot.

"I go no further," said Giant number three and, setting the Drummer down, he strode off as fast as he could.

"Now," thought the Drummer, "so far so good. Here is the Glass Mountain so here, too, must be the Princess," and he began to climb.

Alas, the mountain was truly named, for its surface was as smooth and slippery as glass. No matter how he tried, he slipped back with every step.

"I'll try further on," he thought and took the track that curved around the mountain. He had not gone more than a few paces when he came upon two men arguing angrily about a saddle which lay on the ground before them.

"I have it!"

"No, no, it belongs to me."

"Come now," said the Drummer. "What is all the fuss? I see no horse, so why argue about a saddle?"

"You don't understand," said the first man. "This saddle has magic powers – anyone who sits on it will be transported anywhere at all in the world, simply by wishing."

"No problem there," said the Drummer, running a short distance ahead of them. "See my staff? I will plant it in the ground here. Now I will come back to you and start a race. Whichever of you reaches the staff first, wins the saddle. Ready, steady, go!"

The foolish men obeyed him and as soon as they began to run the Drummer sat on the saddle and, quick as a flash, he'd wished himself to the top of the mountain.

"Now what?" wondered the Drummer, as he looked around the empty plain on the mountain top. All that he could see was an ancient stone mansion. Boldly, the Drummer stepped up to the door and knocked. At the third time of knocking the door was opened by a woman who seemed as ancient as the stones of her house.

"What do you seek?" she asked.

"Provisions and a night's lodging."

"These I can give you, but only if you promise to perform three tasks," said she.

"Why not?" thought the Drummer. "I'm not afraid." So he agreed to the old woman's conditions in return for supper and a good bed.

The next morning the old crone set him the first of his tasks. "Take my thimble and empty the pond of water, take out all the fish and lay them on the bank one by one, all

according to their different kinds. This you must complete before nightfall."

Even though the Drummer set to work, he knew it was useless. By noon when the sun was high he lay exhausted on the grass and the pond was still full. It was then that a young girl came out of the house carrying food for him.

"I see you have worked hard all morning," she said. But the Drummer was in despair. "No matter how hard I work, nothing I can do will save the Princess. I promised to help — even the first of the tasks is too much for me."

"Do not be cast down," said the girl. "Here, rest your head on my lap and sleep. When you wake this work will all be done."

So the Drummer slept and as soon as his eyes closed, the girl turned a wishing ring on her finger and at once the water flew out of the pond and the fish jumped out, each according to its kind, except one which lay apart from the others.

When the Drummer awoke he was truly astonished at what he saw.

"Now," said the girl, "when night comes and the old witch returns you must pick up the fish that lies by itself and throw it in her face crying, 'That is for you, old witch'."

The Drummer did exactly as he was told, but the old woman seemed not to notice his words. She merely smiled grimly and threatened him that his next task would be even harder.

The next day, she gave the Drummer an axe and demanded that he chop down the whole forest, split the wood of the trees into sticks and arrange them into bundles; and all had to be done before nightfall.

Once more the Drummer set to work, but the axe was made of tin and at the first heavy blow it crumpled. As before, he tried by any possible means within his poor strength to accomplish the impossible task but, again, by noon he was close to despair.

Once more the girl appeared with food for him and after he had eaten she commanded him to sleep. Once his eyes closed, she turned her wishing ring and the whole forest came crashing down and arranged itself into bundles of sticks, all except one branch.

"When the old witch appears, you must grasp this branch," said the girl, "and give her one blow with it, saying, 'And this is for you, old witch'."

The Drummer did exactly as she told him but the old witch appeared to feel nothing. She merely laughed and said, "Tomorrow your task will be to pick up all this wood and burn it. See if you can do that before night falls!"

The next morning the Drummer set to work and laboured hard, even though he knew that for one man in one day to pick up a whole forest was not possible. Again, at noon, the girl appeared with food. He ate gratefully and then he slept and while he slept the girl turned her wishing ring and fire glowed within the wood piles and began to consume them one after another, the flames leaping ever higher.

When the Drummer awoke there was nothing before him but the flames still licking the remains of the forest.

"Listen carefully," said the girl. "You must do exactly as I tell you, without fear. If you feel afraid at any time you will

not succeed in rescuing your Princess and you yourself will come to harm. Trust me. When the old witch comes you must do exactly as she tells you – remember, you must do everything she says without fear and, when you have done everything, then you must seize her with both hands and fling her into the fire."

In the evening the old witch returned. She shivered and snivelled and declared how her old bones felt the cold. "It is well that here is fire to warm me enough," she said. "But stay – there in the heart of the fire is a log which will not burn. Fetch it out for me and you will be free to go where you will, but hurry."

Without another thought, the Drummer plunged into the

fire and brought out the log. Not even a hair of his head was singed as he returned triumphant and flung down the log at the old witch's feet. As he did so it was transformed. No sooner had it touched the ground than it turned into the girl who had helped him and, as the Drummer looked at her, he saw she was in truth the beautiful Princess he had promised to help. In wonder he reached out to her, but the old witch leaped between them laughing fiendishly and freezing the Princess where she stood. Just in time the Drummer remembered what he had been told. Seizing the old woman, he flung her away into the flames and at once his Princess was as warm and human as she had been before.

Released from the spell of the Glass Mountain, there was nothing to stop her finding happiness with the Drummer, whose love for her was so great that he had walked through fire for her sake. Gladly the Princess agreed to marry him and they went on their way together, the Drummer drumming for joy at every step.

The Story of the Devil's Bridge

Far beneath the surface of the earth it is very hot. So hot that nothing can possibly live there.

Well, there is someone who lives there. He lives there because he just loves the heat. He's a fat little creature with horns, hooves and a pointed tail. And oh, yes, he is also terribly wicked.

Once upon a very long time ago, this fat little creature woke up shivering. "This hot place is not so hot this morning," he thought.

He looked at the thermometer and found that he was right. "The furnaces must need stoking," he realised. "What I need is a few simple souls to shovel coal. And that means human beings. How can I get humans down here?"

The fat little creature decided that temptation was the answer. He would go up to the surface of the earth and tempt them down with wonderful gifts. "How brilliant I am!" he congratulated himself.

When he arrived on the surface he found himself standing on top of a very high mountain in Wales. He could hear a very strange sound. The fat little creature looked around and saw a humble wood-cutter in the valley below, chopping down a tree with a stone axe.

"Good morning, Sir," called the fat little creature.

Well, the poor wood-cutter was terrified. He thought he was looking at the devil himself — and he was quite right.

"How very hard you have to work, dear Sir," said the little creature, who by now was standing beside the wood-cutter. "What you need is a chain-saw." And, suddenly, a chain-saw appeared in the little Devil's hands. "Now, allow me. And to you, Sir, this wonder tool is absolutely free! All you have to do is sign here on this piece of paper." And he indicated where the wood-cutter was to sign.

"What does it say?" asked the humble wood-cutter, who could neither read nor write.

"It says that you promise to pop down to my place to do some shovelling. Great fun stoking furnaces, you know!"

"I knew there was a catch in it!" said the wood-cutter to himself. "Why, I do believe this one is the Devil! Come to tempt me, he has!"

And turning to the Devil, he said, "No, thank you kindly, but I think I'll stick with the old stone axe." And he turned back to his work of chopping down the tree.

The Devil, seeing that the humble wood-cutter was not to be tempted, decided to go in search of other people. He wandered the Welsh countryside, but no matter where he went, the folk always refused to be tempted. The Devil's hot place, where he returned every night to sleep, grew cooler and cooler.

Then one day, many years later, the Devil saw a fat, jolly cow munching on the side of a steep-sided gorge.

"Oh!" cried the cow. "You gave me such a shock, duckie! Now, I expect you've come to see Megan."

"Who is Megan, Cow?" demanded the Devil.

"You, duckie, may call me Moo; it's short for Moo-Fanwy! Now, that is Megan over there, throwing sticks for her stupid little dog. He's not the sweetest smelling dog in the world, you know. She calls him Pugh, and no wonder! Oh, she's a very simple soul!"

"A simple soul!" cried the Devil excitedly. And he was gone.

"Good morning, ma-am," said the Devil.

"Oh, there's luck for you!" exclaimed Megan. "You're just what I've always wanted! I think I've got just the right spot for you, too. There!" she said, moving the Devil to another place. "That's a good place for a garden gnome! But wait now… how about here… sitting cross-legged… fishing."

"Pardon me, ma-am," said the Devil, "but I think there's some mistake. I am here to offer you a stupendous gift – a

refrigerator! And all you have to do is sign here," he added, holding out a piece of paper.

"Not today, thank you, young man," said Megan. "You disappoint me, you know; you'd make a very good garden gnome! You should think about it!"

The Devil was becoming angry now. "Temper, temper, temper!" warned Moo. "Now, why don't you tempt me, instead?"

"You're no good to me," fumed the Devil. "You're an animal! Animals have four legs and can't shovel! Also, they're not simple souls! Useless!"

"Oh, boo-hoo and boo-hoo again!" answered Moo. "You could have tempted me so easily, too, duckie! I so badly wanted to be able to fly!"

"A cow flying?" laughed the Devil.

"Yes," said Moo. "Then I could fly right across to the other side of this steep gorge and eat that lovely, lovely, lush, green grass."

Well, a flying cow! The Devil was having one of his more wicked ideas.

And, suddenly, before she knew what was happening, Moo was on the other side of the steep gorge.

"Oh, golliwops! Tell me, duckie, how do I get back again?" she asked.

But the fat little creature had gone.

The next morning when Megan went out to milk Moo-Fanwy, she couldn't believe her eyes.

"Gracious!" she said to herself. "How did Moo get over there? Cows can't fly!"

"Good morning, ma-am," said You-Know-Who.

"Away with you!" said Megan crossly. "I've told you once already—I don't need your rubbishy old things!"

"What you need, madam, is a nice little bridge across to the other side."

"You are right!" cried Megan. "But who do I know who could build a bridge?"

"You know little me," answered the sly little Devil.

"But how could a fat little gnome like you ever manage to build a bridge?"

"I-AM-NOT-A-GNOME!"

For a moment, the Devil almost lost his temper. "I build very good bridges, ma-am," he said.

"But I am just a poor old woman with no money at all!" said Megan.

"This bridge will cost you absolutely nothing!" said the Devil eagerly. "Just sign this piece of paper!" And he pushed it at her.

"Oh," said Megan, "I'm afraid I can't read the writing. I left my glasses back in the cottage."

"Just you sign it, dear lady," the Devil simpered, offering her a pen.

And Megan signed.

"By signing this she has agreed that the very first living creature to cross the bridge will shovel coal into my furnaces for ever and ever!" crowed the Devil to himself. "And who will that be? Why, simple old Megan, going over to milk her cow," he answered his own question. "Yuk-Yuk-Yuk!" and he laughed a terrible laugh.

"Now, here it is madam," he said to Megan, "one bridge coming up!"

And, suddenly, there was a bridge across the steep gorge.

"Oh, what a clever little gnome you are!" cried Megan.

The Devil decided not to lose his temper. He watched Megan walk towards the bridge. And she had almost reached it when up rushed little Pugh with a stick in his mouth.

"Now, there's a clever doggie, then," said Megan, bending down to take the stick from Pugh. "Go fetch it, little Pugh!"

And Megan threw the stick – and Pugh went after it.

"Yaaaaaah!!!" screeched the Devil.

"I can't believe it! The first living creature to cross my bridge was a stupid – hairy – smelly – dog!"

"And animals are no good to you, are they, duckie?" laughed Moo. "You told me yourself!"

Well, the Devil was never seen in Wales again, for when he got back to the hot place he found that it had grown so cold that there was only one thing to do – he'd have to stoke those furnaces himself. And there he is to this very day, shovelling, shovelling, shovelling.

Near Aberystwyth in Wales, a very old bridge crosses the river. Above it are two other, newer, bridges. But the lowest one… well, who knows?

It is called Devil's Bridge.

Long, Broad and Quickeye

nce upon a time there was a king who had one son, whom he loved dearly. One day the king sent for his son and said, "My dearest son, my hair is grey and I am old. Soon I shall feel no more the warmth of the sun, nor look upon the trees and flowers. Before I die I would like to see you with a good wife. Marry, my son, as speedily as possible."

"Father," said the prince, "I ask for nothing better than to do your bidding, but I know of no princess whom I could marry."

So the old king took from his pocket a gold key and gave it to his son, saying: "Go up the staircase to the top of the tower. Look carefully round you, and then come to tell me what you like best of all that you see."

The prince had never been in the tower before, and had no idea what he might find. The staircase wound round and round, until he was almost dizzy. At the top he found himself in a hall which had an iron door at one end. He unlocked this door with his golden key, and walked through into a huge room which had a ceiling sprinkled with gold stars, and a carpet of green silk as soft as grass. Twelve windows framed in gold let in the sunlight, and on every window was painted the figure of a young girl, each more beautiful than the last. While the prince gazed at them in surprise, not knowing which he liked best, the girls began to lift their eyes and smile at him. He waited, expecting them to speak, but no sound came.

Suddenly he noticed that one window was covered with a curtain of white silk. He lifted it, and saw before him the image of a young girl as beautiful as the day and as sad as the tomb, clothed in a white dress with a belt of silver and a crown of pearls. The prince stood and looked at her as if he had been turned to stone, and the sadness on her face seemed to pass into his heart. He cried out, "This one shall be my wife. This one and no other."

As he spoke, she blushed and hung her head and the other figures disappeared.

The young prince went quickly back to his father and told him what he had seen and which wife he had chosen. The old man listened to him, full of sorrow, and then he spoke.

"You have done ill, my son, to search out that which was hidden, and you will face great danger. This princess has fallen into the power of a wicked sorcerer who lives in the Iron Castle. Many young men have tried to rescue her, and none have ever come back. But what is done is done! You have given your word. Go, dare your fate, and return to me safe and sound."

So the prince embraced his father, mounted his horse, and set forth to seek his bride. He rode for several hours, until he found himself in a wood where he had never been before, and was soon lost among its winding paths and deep valleys. The thick trees shut out the sun, and he could not tell which was north and which was south. He had given up all hope of getting out of the wood, when he heard a voice calling to him.

"Hey! Hey! Stop a minute!"

The prince turned round and saw a very tall man running towards him.

"Wait for me," he gasped, "and take me into your service.

If you do, you will never be sorry."

"Who are you," asked the prince, "and what can you do?"

"Long is my name, and I can lengthen my body when I choose." And Long showed how he could reach to the top of a tall pine tree and then go back to his normal size.

"Yes, you can do what you say," agreed the prince, "but that's no use to me. Now, if you were only able to get me out of this wood, you would indeed be good for something."

"Oh, that's not difficult," replied Long, and he stretched himself up and up and up until he was three times as tall as the tallest tree in the forest. Then he looked all round and said, "We must go in this direction to get out of the wood." And, shortening himself again, he led the prince's horse along by the bridle.

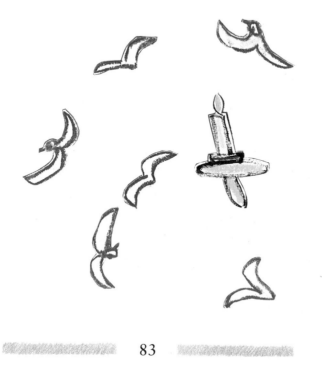

Very soon they were out of the forest and saw before them a wide plain ending in a rising land of high rocks, covered here and there with trees, and what looked very much like the buildings of a distant town.

Long turned to the prince and said, "My Lord, here comes my comrade. You should take him into your service, too, as you will find him a great help."

"Well, call him then, so that I can see what sort of a man he is."

"He is a little too far off for that," replied Long. "He would hardly hear my voice. I think I had better go and bring him myself." This time Long stretched himself to such a height that his head was in the clouds. He made two or three strides, took his friend on his back, and set him down before the prince. The new-comer was a very fat man, as round as a barrel.

"Who are you," asked the prince, "and what can you do?"

"Broad is my name, Sir, and I can make myself as wide as I please. I'll show you. Run, My Lord, as fast as you can, and hide yourself in the wood!" And he began to swell himself up.

The prince saw Long striding towards the wood and decided he had better follow his example. He was only just in time, for Broad had so suddenly inflated himself that he very nearly knocked over the prince and his horse, too. He covered all the space for acres around, as though he were a mountain. Finally Broad stopped expanding, drew a deep breath that made the whole forest tremble, and shrank back down to his usual size.

The prince accepted Broad into his service and the three companions continued on their journey. When they were drawing near the high rocks they met a man whose eyes were covered by a bandage.

"Your Excellency," said Long, "this is our third comrade. You would do well to take him into your service and, I assure you, you would find him worth his salt."

"Who are you?" asked the prince. "And why are your eyes bandaged? You can never see your way!"

"It is just the opposite, My Lord! It is because I see only too well that I am forced to bandage my eyes. When I take the bandage off, my eyes pierce through everything. Everything I look at catches fire or, if it cannot catch fire, it falls into a thousand pieces. They call me Quickeye."

So saying, he took off his bandage and turned towards a rock. As he fixed his eyes upon it a crack was heard and in a few moments it was nothing but a heap of sand. In the sand lay a lump of pure gold, which Quickeye handed to the prince.

"You are a wonderful creature," said the prince, "and I should be a fool not to take you into my service. But, since your eyes are so good, tell me if I am very far from the Iron Castle, and what is happening there."

"If you were travelling alone," replied Quickeye, "it would take you at least one year to reach it but, as we are with you, we shall arrive there tonight. Just now they are preparing supper."

"There is a princess in the castle. Do you see her?"

"A wizard keeps her in a high tower, well guarded by

iron bars."

"Ah, help me to rescue her!" cried the prince.

And they promised they would.

They set out to the Iron Castle and every time they met with an obstacle, one of the three friends contrived somehow to put it aside. As the sun was setting, the prince beheld the towers of the Iron Castle and, before it sank beneath the horizon, he was crossing the iron bridge which led to the

gates. No sooner had the sun disappeared than the bridge drew itself up and the gates clanged shut. There was no turning back.

The prince put his horse in the stable, where everything looked as if a guest was expected, and then they all marched straight up to the castle. In the court, in the stables, and all over the great halls, they saw a number of men richly dressed, but every one turned to stone.

They went through room after room until they reached the dining-hall. It was brilliantly lit and the table was covered with wine and fruit, and was laid for four. They waited a few minutes, expecting someone to come but, as nobody did, they sat down and began to eat and drink, for they were very hungry.

When they had finished, they looked about for a place to

sleep. But suddenly the door burst open, and the wizard entered the hall. He was old and hump-backed, with a bald head and grey beard that fell to his knees. He wore a black robe and, instead of a belt, three iron circlets clasped his waist. He led by the hand a girl of wonderful beauty, dressed in white, with a belt of silver and a crown of pearls, but her face was as pale and sad as death itself.

The prince knew her in an instant, and moved eagerly forward; but the wizard gave him no time to speak, and said, "I know why you are here. You may have her if for three nights you can prevent her making her escape. If you fail in this, you and your servants will all be turned to stone, like those who have come before you." And he left the hall, leaving the princess seated in a chair.

The prince could not take his eyes from the princess. He began to talk to her, but she neither answered nor smiled, only sat as if she were made of marble. He seated himself by her and determined not to close his eyes that night, for fear she should escape. Long stretched himself like a strap all round the room, Broad took his stand by the door and puffed himself out, so that not even a mouse could slip by, and Quickeye leant against a pillar in the middle of the room which supported the roof. But in half a second they were all sound asleep, and they slept the whole night long.

In the morning, at the first peep of dawn, the prince awoke with a start. The princess was gone. He aroused his servants and implored them to tell him what he must do.

"Calm yourself, My Lord," said Quickeye. "I have found her already. A hundred miles from here there is a forest. In the middle of the forest is an old oak tree and, on the top of the oak, an acorn. This acorn is the princess. If Long will take me on his shoulders, we shall soon bring her back." Sure enough, in less time than it takes to walk round a cottage, they had returned from the forest, and Long presented the acorn to the prince.

The prince threw the acorn on the ground, as Quickeye instructed, and the princess appeared at his side.

When the sun peeped for the first time over the mountains, the door burst open as before and the wizard entered, laughing loudly. Suddenly he caught sight of the princess; his face darkened, he uttered a low growl, and one of the iron circlets gave way with a crash. He seized the young girl by the hand and bore her away.

All that day the prince wandered about the castle. Everything looked as if life had suddenly departed. In one place he saw a prince who had been turned to stone in the act of brandishing a sword. In another, the same doom had befallen a knight in the act of running away. In a third, a serving man was standing eternally trying to bring a piece of meat to his mouth. In and around the castle, all was dismal and desolate. Trees there were, but without leaves; fields there were, but no grass grew on them. There was one river, but it never flowed and no fish lived in it. No flowers blossomed, and no birds sang.

Three times during the day food appeared, as if by magic, for the prince and his servants. And it was not until supper was ended that the wizard returned, as on the previous evening, and delivered the princess into the care of the prince.

All four determined that this time they would keep awake at any cost. But it was no use. Off they went to sleep as they had done before, and when the prince awoke the next morning the room was empty again.

With a pang of shame, he rushed to Quickeye. "Awake! Awake! Quickeye! Do you know what has become of the princess?"

Quickeye rubbed his eyes and answered, "Yes, I see her. Two hundred miles from here there is a mountain. In this mountain there is a rock. In the rock, a precious stone. This stone is the princess. Long shall take me there, and we will be back before you can turn round."

So Long took him on his shoulders and they set out. At every stride they covered twenty miles and, as they drew near, Quickeye fixed his burning eyes on the mountain. In an instant it split into a thousand pieces and in one of the pieces sparkled the precious stone. They picked it up and brought it to the prince, who flung it hastily down and, as the stone touched the floor, the princess stood before him.

When the wizard came, his eyes shot forth flames of fury. A cracking noise was heard, and another of his iron bands broke and fell. He seized the princess by the hand and led her off, growling louder than ever.

All that day it was exactly as it had been the day before. After supper the wizard brought back the princess and, looking straight into the prince's eyes, he said, "We shall see which of us will gain the prize after all!"

That night they struggled their very hardest to keep awake, and even walked about instead of sitting down. But it was quite useless. One after another they had to give in, and for the third time the princess slipped through their fingers.

When morning came, once again the prince awoke first and, once again, the princess was gone. The prince rushed to Quickeye.

"Get up Quickeye, and tell me, where is the princess?"

Quickeye looked about for some time without answering. "Oh My Lord, she is far, very far. Three hundred miles away there lies a black sea. In the middle of this sea there is a little shell, and in the middle of the shell is fixed a gold ring. That gold ring is the princess. But do not vex your soul; we will get her. Only, today, Long must take Broad with him."

So Long took Quickeye on one shoulder, and Broad on the other, and they set off. At each stride they left thirty miles behind them. When they reached the black sea, Quickeye showed them the spot where the shell lay. But though Long stretched down his hand as far as it would go, he could not find the shell, for it lay at the bottom of the sea.

Then Broad swelled himself out so that you would have thought the world could hardly have held him and, stooping down, he drank. He drank so much at every mouthful, that only a minute or so had passed before the water had sunk enough for Long to put his hand to the bottom of the sea. He soon found the shell and pulled out the ring.

Time had been lost, and Long had a double burden to carry. The dawn was already breaking before they got back to the castle where the prince was waiting for them in an agony of fear.

Soon the first rays of the sun were seen peeping over the

tops of the mountains. The door burst open and, finding the prince standing alone, the wizard broke into peals of wicked laughter. But as he laughed a loud crash was heard, the window fell into a thousand pieces, a gold ring glittered in the air, and the princess stood before the enchanter.

Quickeye, watching from afar, had told Long of the terrible danger now threatening the prince and Long, summoning all his strength for one gigantic effort, had thrown the ring right through the window.

The wizard shrieked and howled with rage until the whole castle trembled to its foundation. Then another crash was heard, the third iron band split in two, and a black crow flew out the window.

The princess broke the enchanted silence and gave the prince her thanks for rescuing her.

It was not only the princess who was restored to life by the flight of the black crow. The marble figures became men once more and took up their occupations just as they had left them. The horses neighed in the stables, the flowers blossomed in the garden, the birds flew in the air, the fish darted in the water. Everywhere, all was life and joy.

The knights who had been turned to stone came in a body to offer their homage to the prince who had set them free.

"Do not thank me," he said, "for I have done nothing. Without my faithful servants, Long, Broad and Quickeye, I should have been as one of you."

With these words he bade them farewell, and departed with the princess and his faithful companions for the kingdom of his father.

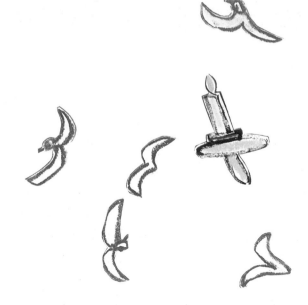

The old king, who had long since given up all hope, wept for joy at the sight of his son, and insisted that the wedding should take place as soon as possible.

All the knights who had been enchanted in the Iron Castle were invited to the ceremony and then Long, Broad and Quickeye took leave of the young couple, saying that they were going to look for more work.

The prince tried to persuade them to stay and offered them all their hearts could desire, but they replied that an idle life would not please them, and that they could never be happy unless they were busy. So they went away to seek their fortunes, and they are probably seeking them still.

The Sharpest Witch

There was a miller who was made of wheat, and he was travelling through the countryside in his cart, pulled by his horse, who was made of straw. And as he clip-clopped along, the miller told this tale:

'Once upon a time, in this very village, a strange thing happened very suddenly. All the crops rotted and died, so there was little food, and the animals all grew sick. No one knew what to do, for no one knew what had caused this to happen.

There was a witch who lived in the village. She loved to cook, and she had mixers and whisks and microwaves and dishwashers, for she was a modern witch, made of metal, who knew all about saving time by using appliances and technology. One day the metallic witch was cleaning her whisk and saying,

> "No ice cream or lollipops,
> Otherwise my battery stops."

"Ohh, my stomach aches." She chanted as she looked through her small, leather spell book,

> "To eat some children soon I must,
> For if I don't my parts will rust.
> Now to devise a wonderful plan,
> To catch those children for my favourite flan."

And she opened the doors to a huge cupboard, which was packed with aerosol sprays.

> "Pesticide, herbicide,
> Fungicide, insecticide..."

At midnight the metallic witch was on her vacuum cleaner, which she used instead of a broomstick, flying over the sleeping village, spraying aerosols, casting her wicked spell.

"Children, children, tender meat,
I'll cast this spell and have you to eat."

Smoke filled the air as the witch flew off home, her spell cast and the damage done, as all the trees and the fruit began to rot.

The next day, Annie, one of the village children, picked an apple from a tree that still looked healthy, even though it was dying. As she looked at the apple, a juicy, fat worm wriggled out. "Yuk!" Annie threw the apple on the ground and it rolled towards a stream, where dead fish were floating. As Annie watched, more apples fell from the tree into the water, and each had worms and insects crawling out.

Nearby, Annie's brother Tom was digging for vegetables, but each one that he dug up was bad. He threw down a carrot that he was holding and sighed.

Just then, Annie and Tom heard the familiar sound of the miller's horse and cart approaching. "Gran, Gran, the miller's here!" called Annie.

The children's grandmother put aside her sewing and stood up from her rocking chair in the kitchen. The news on the radio was just ending. "Today, we are no closer to solving the mystery of the disease that is ruining the crops and killing the animals." Gran sighed, as well, and went out to meet the miller.

"Enough for only one small loaf, I'm afraid," he told her as he handed her a small bag of flour.

She shook her head and sighed. "What shall we do?"

"I don't know what's happening in this village," he answered, "but if the crops don't start growing soon, we're all going to starve."

"We shall have to go into the forest tomorrow and search for berries and nuts," declared Tom to Annie.

The next morning, Gran cut the small loaf she had baked into three pieces and gave them each a slice. "Now, make this last as long as you can, " she advised them. "And take these red ribbons with you. Tie them to the tree boughs as you go, so they can help you find your way home. Remember, don't stray from the path! Goodbye, children."

The children hugged their grandmother and set off.

Tom tied bows to the branches as he went. Annie searched for berries, nuts and mushrooms, but found only rotten fruit. They hunted all day and when night fell, they made a fire from twigs and ate their last crust.

"What are we going to do?" Annie asked Tom. "We've been here all day and we haven't found a single berry."

Tom shrugged. "We'll have to go deeper into the forest when it gets light."

Just as he finished speaking, a roaring sound filled the air. The trees around them began to swell until they were ten times their normal size, and all the plants and bushes changed colours and glowed fierce reds and oranges. Then the plants began to whip and lash at Annie and Tom, who were trying to hide under Annie's shawl.

Suddenly, the noise stopped and the forest became normal again. Annie peeped out. "Look, Tom."

"It must be the sun coming up," said Tom, seeing something flickering in the trees.

No sooner had Tom said this, than a giant butterfly fluttered past, its wings a tapestry of yellow, scarlet, purple and black. The children watched it with wonder, and then got up and raced after it, going deeper and deeper into the forest.

"Oh, Tom, I can't run any more!" cried Annie finally.

"Neither can I," panted Tom. "We've lost it, anyway." And the children leaned over with their hands on their knees to catch their breath.

When they stood up, they couldn't believe their eyes. There was the most wonderful and delicious-looking palace before them. It was made of candy canes, juicy fruits and sugar spices, with balloons of every colour and shape surrounding it. The children licked their lips hungrily.

"Oh!" said Tom. "I can smell pizza. And look, there's ice cream, too. Come on, let's eat!"

The children ran up to the house and ate as much as they could. The window panes were made of toffee; mozzerella cheese dripped from the pizza roof; a stream of raspberry ice cream flowed from the water pump.

A sign over a doorway read 'Good Eat' and the butterfly they had chased fluttered below it. Suddenly the butterfly spoke. "Do come in, children. The food is even better inside."

The children walked into the palace. The walls sparkled with rainbow coloured fruitdrops and clouds of candy floss hovered over their heads.

"Ooh, it's lovely!" exclaimed Annie.

"Delicious," agreed Tom, eating again.

The children had just climbed on to two sugar candy rocking horses, when the butterfly flew before them. "Can I take your order?"

Tom and Annie looked at each other and then spoke to the butterfly. "But we don't have any money."

"You don't need any here."

"Then I'll have a big, juicy, fat hot dog dripping with tomato ketchup," smiled Tom.

"And I'll have a meaty hamburger smothered in mustard," added Annie.

The butterfly fluttered off, and went straight to the modern witch's kitchen, for this palace was her creation. The witch's appliances were already hard at work, food processors chopping and mixers blending. Suddenly there was a flash of light and the butterfly turned into the metallic witch herself, who cackled as she began to prepare Tom and Annie's order.

> "Those tasty mortals do not know,
> It's I who'll not allow the crops to grow.
> So when they come in search of wheat,
> They're captured by my candy treats.
> This food shall be their very last,
> For I must eat them pretty fast."

The butterfly soon fluttered over to the children, with the food flying in front. They were delighted.

"Mmm!" said Annie.

Just as the children were about to take a bite, there was a crash of thunder and a flash of light and there stood the witch. The stunned children did not have time to move as metal grips descended and grasped them. They were lifted up, screaming in terror.

The grips held them tightly by their trousers, suspended

over a huge cooking wok, where the witch began cooking up a soup, all her modern appliances whirring. She turned on the video as she switched on the television, to record her favourite cookery program with a cookery witch. She was just in time.

"Lovely 'spiced children' we're cooking today,
Perfect for taking those rumbles away."

The witch emptied cans of oil and petrol into the wok, adding bits of bone and glass that the recipe called for.

"Cook them up in rich black oil,
Keep on stirring till they boil."

The witch tested the temperature with her cooking

thermometer, licking off the inky oil.

"Rich, oily soup, delicious taste.
Now eggs and flour to make the paste."

With a cackle, the witch lowered Tom into a cooking pot, brushed him with egg yolk and sprinkled him with flour. She lowered Annie and released her, saying,

"Little mortal, your help I need.
Set the table for me to feed."

Annie, surprised, set the table, apart from a spoon. The witch continued,

"To the dishwasher, there you'll find,
The largest spoon of its kind."

But Annie hid the spoon behind her back, and said, "But, Witch, there is no spoon to be seen. Are you sure it's here?"
The witch pushed Annie aside.

"Stupid child, I'll find the spoon,
Then I shall dine very soon."

And she put her head in the dishwasher to see better as she rummaged about. Annie slowly moved behind the witch and slapped her with the spoon so that the witch fell into the dishwasher. Annie slammed the door and started the machine. She could hear the witch screaming, and the machine was shaking.

Tom jumped down from the cooking pot where he'd been standing, sneezing from the flour.

The children opened the dishwasher. All they could see was a few nuts and bolts and rusting bits of metal. At once, fruit began to grow all around the kitchen.

Tom and Annie walked home through the forest. Annie picked fruit for their grandmother as Tom untied the red ribbon. They saw the miller on their way, who tipped his hat to the children.'

And so the miller was able to end his tale:

'So, Annie and Tom returned home safely. And that very same day, leaves appeared on the trees and the crops began to grow again. The village slowly returned to normal but, still, people speak of the time when the crops failed. No one could explain it, and the mystery is still unsolved.'

Beauty Pinkerton and the Spiny Legged Wart Groveller

Jeremiah Pinkerton was a very rich man who lived in a huge mansion with his family. Every day when he came home from work he brought a rosebud for his youngest daughter, Beauty. His other children demanded more expensive presents. "Pearls!" cried one daughter. "And a new dress!" demanded another.

One terrible day, Jeremiah lost all his money. His family had to move from their great mansion to a dingy shack in Tintown. It was terribly noisy whenever it rained because the houses were all made of corrugated iron. And it seemed to rain all the time in Tintown.

Jeremiah's grumpy children went to bed. "And we're not getting up until we're rich again!" they announced. But not Beauty. She didn't go to bed; she cheered herself up by playing her favourite record by Trevor Prince, a singer who had disappeared mysteriously a few years before.

Life became hard. One afternoon Jeremiah sat in the Candy Castle Cafe, moaning into a cup of tea. "I haven't even got enough money to buy Beauty her rosebud."

He looked up to see if anyone had overheard him and saw, on the table before him, a plastic rosebud in a glass. Quickly, he snatched it. As he did so, the front door of the cafe slammed shut and locked. Jeremiah was trapped.

"Where do you suppose
You're taking my rose?"

growled a voice behind him. Jeremiah whirled round and squealed in fear. An ugly monster stood growling at him; it was the dreadful Spiny Legged Wart Groveller – known as

Spiny, for short.

> "Those who steal must make a deal,
> Or else I'll have to make them squeal,"

threatened Spiny.

"But I've got nothing to give you," the terrified Jeremiah managed to say. And then he found himself telling this stranger his whole story. A beast with a heart of ice could resist such a sorrowful story, but Spiny couldn't. He said,

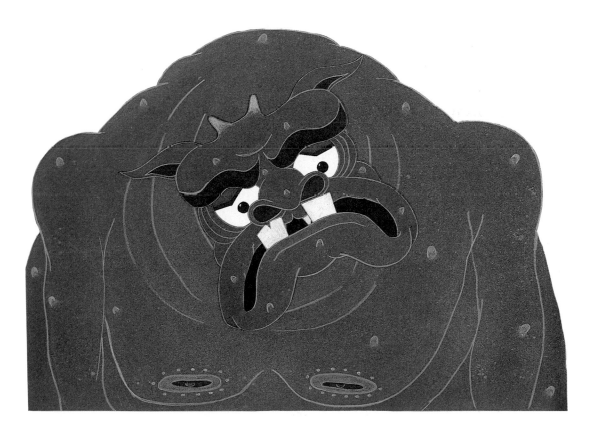

> "Bring your daughter to stay with me
> And I'll spare your life and let you be."

Jeremiah had to agree to this. Spiny put him into a big black car and sent him back to Tintown to collect Beauty.

His greedy children heard the big car arrive and were delighted. "We're rich again!" they cried and rushed outside to greet their father. They were met by a gloomy face and awful news that sent them howling back to their beds.

Poor Beauty was very upset. "I have to go to the beast to save Father," she thought, so she kissed her brothers and sisters goodbye and climbed into the waiting car, which took her and Jeremiah back to Candy Castle.

They went inside to wait. Soon, doors to a lift opened, revealing a creature far uglier than any Beauty had expected. But she remained calm, not showing her fear.

Spiny greeted her with,

> "Beauty, when you came today
> Did you know you'd have to stay?"

In a shaky voice, Beauty whispered, "Yes."
So Spiny said to Jeremiah,

> "Take the car, now full of treasure,
> For Beauty, I have paid full measure."

Jeremiah left, and Beauty cried herself to sleep in the room that was hers. As she slept, she dreamed of her idol, Trevor Prince, who sang to her,

"Don't be fooled by appearances,
For nothing is as it seems,
Only you can save me,
Believe in your dreams."

Beauty was just about to ask what he meant when she woke. She was very confused. "Is Trevor a prisoner, too?" she thought. "If so, I must find him and rescue him!"

Beauty began to search the castle. She didn't find Trevor but she did discover what a magical place Candy Castle was. Each room she entered was more wondrous than the last. At the end of the day, Beauty was so tired that she was glad to find Spiny waiting with her supper.

As they ate, they talked, and Beauty realised that Spiny

wasn't as frightening as she had first thought but, when he asked her if she could ever love him, Beauty was scared. Spiny urged her to answer truthfully, so Beauty said "No."

As she slept that night, Beauty again dreamed of Trevor. And he sang to her,

> "Don't be unkind and fill me with dread,
> Think with your heart and not with your head."

When she awoke, Beauty was determined to find Trevor, but each day brought the same routine. Beauty opened many doors in the castle, but Trevor was never behind one.

And every night Spiny asked, "Could you ever love me?"

And every night Beauty answered "No," and then dreamed of Trevor, singing,

> "Don't be fooled by appearances,
> For..."

And at this point Beauty would kiss him.

Beauty began to miss her family, so one night she asked Spiny if she could visit them.

He said,

> "If you hate me so much,
> Then you must go;
> I love you so much,
> That I can't say 'no'."

Beauty replied, "I don't hate you. I just miss my family. If you let me go for two months, I promise I'll come back."

> "Go to sleep and when you wake,
> You'll find yourself at home;
> Remember that my heart will break,
> If you don't return.
> In two months' time take this ring,
> And turn it on your thumb,
> Say 'I must see my beast again',
> And back to me you'll come.
> Goodnight, Beauty."

Sure enough, Beauty woke to find herself back with her family, who were very pleased to see her. Even so, she still dreamed of Trevor. One day she asked Jeremiah what he thought her dreams meant.

"It could be that Trevor is talking about Spiny, and is telling you that although he's ugly, his heart is good."

Now, this set Beauty thinking about Spiny and the enjoyable evenings that she had spent with him. But she let the two months pass because it was difficult to say goodbye to her family.

One night, in a terrible dream, Beauty found Spiny lying under a tree, looking very ill. He whispered to her, "See what

happens when people break their promises."

Beauty was very scared. She turned the ring on her thumb and said, "I wish to see my Spiny again."

The next morning when she awoke she was back in Candy Castle. She quickly ran out to the garden and found Spiny just as she'd seen him in the dream.

"Why, oh why didn't I keep my promise?" she cried, and some of her tears fell on to Spiny's face. Suddenly his chest heaved, his eyes opened and he smiled at her.

"You're alive!" cried Beauty joyfully.

"Yes, Beauty, your tears have saved me. Do you love me, will you marry me?"

"When I thought that I might have lost you," Beauty told him, "I realised that I do love you and, yes, I will marry you!"

Suddenly, there was a flash of light and, where Spiny had been, stood Trevor Prince.

"I once refused to marry an evil old witch called Yaggot," he explained. "She screamed that if she couldn't have me, then no one would. I instantly found myself here at Candy Castle, transformed into the Spiny Legged Wart Groveller that you once knew. The only thing that could break the evil old witch's spell was for someone to love me and agree to marry me as I was. You, my Beauty, did just that."

And so the next day's headlines ran, 'TREVOR PRINCE FOUND!' The news soon spread throughout the country and Beauty and Trevor's wedding was a splendid affair.

They returned to Candy Castle and, not surprisingly, lived happily ever after.

Jack and the Beanstalk

Jack and his mother were poor. They lived alone in a basement flat in the middle of a great city. Behind the flat was a tiny yard, and in the tiny yard there was a patch of grass. On this grass they kept a cow which they called Milky White.

The sun had always shone in the yard, until building began next door. The tower that was built was so tall that its top was always hidden by clouds. It blocked out all the sunlight in the tiny yard and so the grass turned yellow, shrivelled and stopped growing. Poor Milky White!

One morning Jack was flicking channels on the television when his mother said, "Jack, there's no grass left for Milky White and we can't afford to feed her. While I'm at work you must take her to the street market and try to sell her." She kissed Jack and hurried away, saying, "Get as much money as you can for Milky White."

Jack was terribly sad at the thought of losing Milky White, but he knew how poor they were. "I'll have to sell her," he thought miserably.

He led the cow along the crowded city pavement, but before he reached the street market he met an old man. Jack looked twice, because the old man was playing a harp – a magical harp, with arms and a head. "I can't trade you this harp for your cow," said the old man, "because I'd be lost without it. But I'll give you this tin of beans for your cow," he offered, and then he grinned and winked. "They are magic beans."

Magic or not, it was a large tin of beans, easily enough for two meals. Jack looked at Milky White and then at the beans again. "It's still a long walk to market," he thought, eyeing the tin.

"All right," he said and, leaving Milky White with her new owner, he sadly set off for home with the beans.

When Jack got home he decided to cook the dinner as a surprise for his mother. The beans were in a pan, simmering on the cooker, when he heard his mother at the door.

"What did you get?" asked his mother excitedly.

"Beans!" grinned Jack.

But Jack's mother did not smile. "Idiot!" she shouted. She flung the beans out the window and they landed in the yard where Milky White used to graze.

Jack was sent to bed without even a bean for his supper. He woke early the next morning with a rumbling stomach. "I could eat that whole tin of beans by myself," he thought hungrily.

He jumped out of bed and then he saw, outside his window, right there where the beans had landed in the tiny yard, the tallest, strangest plant he had ever seen. It was purple and covered in spots and it was as tall as the building next door. The top of it disappeared into the clouds.

"Wow!" gasped Jack. "I'll climb it," and, still in his pyjamas, he went through his bedroom window on to the plant.

He climbed and he climbed and he climbed. He climbed past all the windows of the tall building next door; past all the amazed faces of the people inside who saw him go by.

Up through the clouds Jack climbed until he came to a large orange flower right at the top of the beanstalk. Jack

looked at the building next to him and saw that the top of it was a castle, with pointed turrets and a huge door.

"This has got to be a giant's castle!" exclaimed Jack.

He crawled along a shoot of the beanstalk and knocked at the door. The door opened suddenly from the top, dropping like a drawbridge, and hit Jack on the head.

"Ouch!" he said just as a tall woman with a green face and a broad smile looked out.

"Yes? Is someone here?" she asked. Jack crawled out from under the door.

As usual, Jack thought of his stomach first. "Could you spare a piece of toast for breakfast, please?" he asked hopefully.

The woman looked down at him. "My husband will be home soon," she boomed. "He eats boys like you for breakfast."

"But I've climbed a very long way and I haven't eaten for ages."

"You'll have to be quick then," she chuckled, "or *you'll* be breakfast!"

Jack had to run to keep up as she walked away.

Seated on a giant-sized overturned cup inside the castle, Jack was given two giant-sized pieces of toast. He had only taken two normal-sized bites when there was a 'Ping!' and, on the other side of the room, doors to a lift opened. Jack saw a green giant squashed into the lift, sitting cross-legged on the floor.

"Fee, fi, fo, fum, I smell the blood of an Englishman...!" the giant roared. Jack could hear giant-sized footsteps pounding closer. "...Be he alive or be he dead, I'll grind his bones to make my bread!"

"Quick!" whispered the giant's wife. "Hide in the oven!" Jack ran towards the oven, dragging a piece of toast with him, and hopped inside.

"There's no one here but me, dear," said the giant's wife, loudly. "Come and eat your breakfast."

Jack could see the giant eating his giant-sized breakfast through the oven's glass door. When he had finished, the giant opened a bag and began to count the money that he had stolen in the city the night before. In no time, the giant's head crashed on to the table and he was fast asleep.

Quick as a flash, Jack leaped out of the oven, snatched as much money as he could carry, ran out of the castle and climbed down the beanstalk as fast as he could go.

"This time Mother will be pleased!" he thought.

His mother was not the only one who was pleased. The mayor of the city was delighted to have some of the stolen money returned, and he rewarded honest Jack handsomely. Jack was a hero. His picture was in all the papers and he took his mother on a trip around the world.

But when they returned, all their money was gone. They were as poor as before. "I'll climb the beanstalk once again," decided Jack.

Once again he climbed above the clouds and knocked at the castle door. Jack remembered that the door worked like a drawbridge, and stepped to one side. But, this time, the door opened sideways, like a normal door, and Jack was squashed flat behind it.

Once again the giant's wife with the green face and the broad smile answered, "Hello? Is anyone here?"

Jack stepped from behind the door. "Could you spare a piece of toast for breakfast, please?"

"I really shouldn't be doing this," said the giant's wife, leading him into the kitchen and handing him the giant-sized toast. "Some money went missing last time you were here. If my husband comes back he'll. . ."

'Ping!' The lift had arrived, and the giant with it. "Fee, fi, fo, fum, I smell the blood of an Englishman!" he roared.

Jack headed straight for the oven.

The pounding giant-sized footsteps grew louder. "Be he alive or be he dead, I'll grind his bones to make my bread!"

"There's no one here but me, dear," said the giant's wife.

"Good. Cook this for my dinner!" boomed the giant, handing his wife a hen.

Jack watched while the giant left the room and his wife went to get a saucepan. Then, as quickly as he could, he darted out from the oven, grabbed the hen and was out the door in no time. He could hear the giant's wife saying,

"Where's it gone?" as he started down the beanstalk.

Now Jack didn't know it, but this hen was no ordinary hen. She layed golden eggs. She lived happily in the tiny yard where Milky White once grazed, strutting around the yard laying lots of golden eggs. Jack and his mother were no longer poor and, thanks to their generosity, neither were their friends and neighbours.

But, one day, out of curiosity, Jack decided to climb the beanstalk one more time.

Up above the clouds he climbed, and knocked at the castle door. He remembered how the door opened and jumped to the side. But the door swung open the other way and squashed Jack behind it. "Ouch!" he yelled.

The giant's wife was not pleased to see him when he crawled out. "Go away!" she said and slammed the door, so Jack climbed in through the window and hid anyway.

Once again Jack heard the familiar 'Ping!' as the giant arrived home. But the giant's wife was surprised to hear him say, "Fee, fi, fo, fum, I smell the blood of an Englishman! Be he alive or be he dead, I'll grind his bones to make my bread!"

The giant's wife smiled at her husband. "Well, dear, if he is here, he'll be hiding in the oven. I've switched it on; you can have him for breakfast."

The giant smiled and said to his wife, "Look what I've found!" and there was the magic harp that belonged to the old man.

"Play!" commanded the giant, and the harp played. In no time, the giant was sleeping.

Luckily, Jack had not hidden in the oven this time. He

crawled out from underneath a bowl, seized the magic harp and ran. Only, this time, the giant awoke. "I'll get you this time!" he roared. Jack raced down the beanstalk with the giant clambering after him.

But the giant was giant-sized and clumsy. He wasn't used to climbing beanstalks; he was used to taking the lift. As Jack nimbly climbed down and reached the bottom, the giant grew more and more uncertain and, with a cry, he lost his grip on the stalk and fell to the ground. Jack and his mother watched helplessly as the giant fell.

Jack had saved the city. He returned the magic harp to the old man. Thanks to the hen, Jack and his mother weren't poor anymore and they lived happily ever after. . .and so did everyone else.